Selkies (seals who can shed their skins to take human form on land) are a classic part of Scottish mythology. They often appear in stories from around the north coast of Scotland.

I dedicate this book to my dear friend Dawn, with love – J.M.

*To Captain K , Miss W, CO, Scruffy and all my friends who
belong to faraway worlds – R.M.*

THIS BOOK BELONGS TO

_____

_____

The Selkie Girl

Retold by Janis Mackay

Illustrated by Ruchi Mhasane

Fergus was the son of a poor widower fisherman. They lived
in a lonely cottage down by the Scottish shore. They were
happy enough, though Fergus's father did not catch as many
fish as he used to, and Fergus missed his mother.

Fergus spent long hours alone beach-combing. He found
special shells, fossils, driftwood, coloured glass and stones.
He brought his findings home to cheer up the little cottage.

Once he found a starfish with no legs missing. Once he found a shell with the sound of the sea in it. And once he found an old copper coin.

"Look!" he said proudly to his father. "Treasures!"

"Aye, son," the fisherman said kindly, though it was fish he wished for.

On midsummer's day, the longest day of the year, Fergus wandered far along the shore to some craggy rocks. Beyond them lay a beautiful secret bay, which was usually cut off by the tide.

But on this day his luck was in. The tide was out.

Fergus scrambled his way round to the secret beach. The shimmer of golden sand swept his breath away. He felt scared and excited at the same time. Squinting into the sun, he could make out a silhouette at the far end of the beach. What was it? A tree? A standing stone?

Fergus had no time to find out. The tide was turning and soon the waves would swallow up the golden sand. He would be trapped!

He spotted a piece of smooth fur draped over a stone, and ran over for a closer look. The dark shiny fur was speckled with silver. He had never seen anything like it. It felt warm and soft to touch.

"Treasure!" he cried and snatched it up.

Fergus didn't see the girl in the distance running towards him, her arms waving wildly in the air.

Fergus threw the precious fur over his shoulder and ran. There was no time to lose. Waves were whipping round his ankles and snaking round his legs. A seagull, or something that sounded like a seagull, screeched at his back. Panting hard, Fergus reached the craggy rocks. He waded round to the safety of the open shore.

With his heart pounding, he climbed the grassy path. He didn't notice the large seal in the bay honking desperately at him. Nor did he see the girl with the long brown hair down on the secret beach, or hear her cries. Clambering up the path, he shook out the prized fur. It flapped in the breeze like a flag. What a find!

The girl down on the secret beach searched frantically for her seal skin. She was a selkie – half human, half seal. To return to the sea, she needed her skin. It was as precious to her as her beating heart. Her mother honked loudly from the sea, warning her to return.

The girl's seal skin was gone. Soon the beach would be gone. She plunged into the incoming waves and swam as hard as she could. Human swimming was difficult and dangerous. It was hard to swim with no flippers and tail fins. It was hard to swim with no seal skin.

Exhausted, the girl crawled ashore on a stony beach. She knew little about humans, but knew they wore clothes. She found a tangled fishing net on the beach and wrapped it around herself. She came across a torn old jacket snagged on a rock and put that on too. Seaweed clung to her hair.

The seal-girl sniffed the wind. Her seal skin was nearby,
she was sure. Where had that boy taken it?
    She gazed out to sea. Her mother was out there somewhere.
Shivering with cold, and afraid humans might see her, the girl
hid under an upturned fishing boat. The lapping song of the sea
lulled her to sleep.

The next morning, Fergus laid out the fur along with his other treasures. It was the best thing he had ever found. He wanted to show it to the children up in the village. He was sure that then they would be his friends.

Suddenly he heard a banging at the window behind him.

"That is my skin!" cried a voice from outside.

Fergus swung round. A wild girl with seaweed in her
hair was staring at him through the window. Again she
banged on the glass, so hard Fergus was sure it would break.
"I am a selkie," she cried. "I can't go home without my
seal skin. Give it back to me!"

The girl ran into the room.

"You stole my seal skin!"

Fergus stared at her. Could it be true? He had heard the stories of selkies – magical seals that could take off their skins and change into humans.

"Stay!" he blurted out, the seal skin clutched behind his back. "Be my friend... please!"

The seal-girl shook her head. "I can't," she sobbed, "I live under the sea."

"If you stay," whispered Fergus, "after seven days, I'll give the skin back."

So the girl wiped her tears and nodded. "My name is Shonagh," she said.

"I'm Fergus," he said, smiling.

Shonagh refused to stay in the house, so Fergus brought blankets and cushions for her boat-house. He brought her an old blue dress that had been his mother's.

Shonagh said she felt strange in a dress.

They played tig on the beach. It was windy, so Fergus brought out his kite and taught Shonagh how to fly it.

"I like playing on land," she told him. "It's fun!"

And the kite flew high in the blue sky.

Shonagh showed Fergus how to catch fish with his bare hands. Their laughter drifted on the summer breeze. And when the sun went down, Fergus and Shonagh gathered driftwood and made a fire on the beach. They toasted bannocks and ate them.

"They're tasty," said Shonagh, licking her lips, "but I prefer fish."

"Stay for ever," Fergus said. It felt so good to have a friend. But the selkie girl gazed out to sea and shook her head.

Fergus's father complained that he was catching no fish at all these days.

"You'd think the sea had put a curse on me," he grumbled. But he was surprised, and happy, when Fergus brought home a huge pile of fish for their dinner.

"I caught all these," Fergus told his dad proudly, "with my bare hands."

And a rare smile passed across his father's face.

"Perhaps," he said, "our luck has turned."

The week passed quickly. The seventh day dawned. Fergus felt sad, but he kept his promise. Down on the beach he gave Shonagh back her seal skin. She gave him a small pink stone.

"It's a friendship stone," she said, pressing it gently into his palm. "I will never forget you, Fergus, my human friend."

Shonagh wrapped the seal skin around her shoulders. She waved to Fergus, then turned and dived into the sea.

Moments later, a beautiful seal lifted its sleek dark head from the sparkling water. Looking directly at Fergus, the seal lifted a flipper and softly honked.

"Goodbye!" called Fergus.

Shonagh kept her promise. She never did forget Fergus.
Every night, his father's fishing nets were full. There was
more than enough for Fergus and his father. They invited
people from the village to share dinner with them.
The friends told stories round the flickering peat fire, long
into the night. And each morning Fergus's father sailed
out to sea with a smile on his face.

Fergus missed Shonagh – but the children in the village had seen him flying his kite, and came to ask if they could fly it with him.

Fergus showed his new friends how to build a bonfire, and caught fish for them with his bare hands. And sometimes, while the children played around the beach fire together, Fergus could see Shonagh out at sea, watching him.

Perhaps one day, you will see her too.